SECOND CHANCE RANCH

IT'S NOT DESTINY

AN ABBY STORY

Book design by Jake Nordby
Illustrations by Jomike Tejido

Published in the United States by Jolly Fish Press, an imprint of North Star Editions, Inc.

First Edition
First Printing, 2018

This is a work of fiction. Names, characters, places, and incidents are either the product of the author's imagination or are used fictitiously, and any resemblance to actual persons living or dead, business establishments, events, or locales is entirely coincidental.

Library of Congress Cataloging-in-Publication Data (pending)
978-1-63163-145-0 (paperback)
978-1-63163-144-3 (hardcover)

Jolly Fish Press
North Star Editions, Inc.
2297 Waters Drive
Mendota Heights, MN 55120
www.jollyfishpress.com

Printed in the United States of America

SECOND CHANCE
RANCH

IT'S NOT DESTINY

AN ABBY STORY

KELSEY ABRAMS

ILLUSTRATED BY JOMIKE TEJIDO

TEXT BY WHITNEY SANDERSON

JOLLY
FiSH
PRESS

Mendota Heights, Minnesota

Chapter One

"Abby, are you ready to give your presentation to the class?" Mr. Timothy, Abby's fifth-grade teacher, asked.

Abby took a deep breath and reached down to put a hand on Amigo's head. But Amigo wasn't there. Amigo had been Abby's service dog since first grade, but for the last month, she had been going to school without him.

Amigo was ten years old, which was seventy in dog years. Lately, he'd been acting kind of sleepy and slow. Abby's mother, a veterinarian, had diagnosed him with a heart murmur and given him some medication. She had said it would make him feel more comfortable—but it wouldn't cure him. Amigo was just getting old.

It had been a hard choice, but Abby had decided not to take him to school anymore. That was a big change, and Abby didn't like change. She liked routines. She even had a chart on the wall in her room that helped remind her of her morning routine, from brushing her teeth to making sure her homework was packed. If anything unusual was happening that day, like a field trip or a doctor's appointment, Abby wrote it on her chart the night before.

Abby even liked to have the same breakfast every

morning: a banana, peanut butter on toast, and a glass of orange juice. If they were out of bananas or only had apple juice, Abby's day just didn't feel the same.

Putting on Amigo's service dog vest and getting him ready to go to school each morning had been Abby's favorite part of her routine. Not having him with her felt a lot worse than having apple juice for breakfast instead of orange.

The reason Abby had a service dog was because she had autism, which meant she sometimes had trouble communicating her feelings and reading other people's emotions. She also got anxious about things like loud noises or crowds of people or having to look people in the eye when she talked to them. Having Amigo around helped keep Abby calm and gave her something to focus on when it felt like the whole world was melting into a meaningless blur of color and sound.

"I'm ready, Mr. Timothy," said Abby, even though it was only about 60 percent true. She gathered her notes and walked slowly to the whiteboard at the front of the class.

Abby knew some other people with autism, like Jack from her playgroup when she was younger, who didn't talk at all but pointed to pictures to communicate. Abby could talk just fine; according to her three sisters, she often overdid the talking. In fact, most people probably wouldn't have known that Abby had autism at all. Sometimes that made things harder because people didn't understand why she got so anxious about some things, like school presentations.

Of course, that might have had nothing to do with autism. Abby's friend Miriam didn't have autism, and she was even more nervous about presentations than Abby was. Earlier that year, Miriam had had to read her book report on *Charlotte's Web* in front of the class. When she'd opened her mouth to begin, her voice had come out as a little *squeak*, like a mouse. It had been really funny, but Abby hadn't laughed, because she'd known Miriam hadn't thought it was funny at all. Back in first grade or maybe even second, Abby probably would have laughed. But she'd learned a lot since then.

If Amigo was beside her now, Abby would have imagined that everyone was admiring him instead of looking at her. And Amigo was such a handsome dog that it probably would have been true. Since he wasn't there, Abby decided to imagine that she was already grown up and a famous scientist, giving a lecture to her colleagues.

"This is Dr. Abby Ramirez," she began.

The class rippled with laughter. Abby blushed. She hadn't meant to share what she was imagining with the class. Mr. Timothy put a finger to his lips and then to his ear, telling the class to be quiet and listen.

"I mean, this is Abby Ramirez," she corrected. "My report is on the training of sled dogs for the Iditarod. The Iditarod is a one-thousand-mile race from Settler's Bay to Nome in Alaska. In 1925, there was an outbreak of diphtheria in Nome, but bad weather prevented trains, ships, and airplanes from delivering the serum that cured the disease. Relay teams of sled dogs, however, were able to cover the

distance and deliver the medicine to Nome. The modern Iditarod is run in commemoration of that event."

As Abby went on, she felt her tense muscles relax. She realized that she'd been flapping her left hand in rhythm with her speech, which she sometimes did when she was nervous. If Amigo had been there, he would have given her a gentle nudge with his nose to let her know what she was doing. Abby was proud of herself for noticing it on her own.

She took her notes in both hands and continued. "Each team consists of sixteen sled dogs and one musher, or driver. Alaskan huskies are the most popular sled dog breed. Sled dogs usually begin their training at around nine months old . . ."

When Abby reached the end of her report, everyone in the class clapped without being told.

"Nice job, Abby," said Mr. Timothy. "That was a very thorough report."

As Abby headed back to her desk, Miriam gave her a thumbs-up.

"Was it overkill?" Abby asked her after class, pushing Miriam's wheelchair as they headed to the cafeteria for lunch. Miriam's wheelchair had a remote control that allowed her to go wherever she wanted on her own, but Abby liked pushing it, and Miriam let her.

"No, I don't think it was overkill," said Miriam, to Abby's relief.

Sometimes Abby got so interested in topics that she kept talking about them long after other people's attention started to wander. But Miriam loved dogs nearly as much as Abby, so she didn't mind long conversations about them. In fact, that was how they'd become friends.

Abby hadn't made any friends at all in kindergarten. Mostly she'd played by herself with her favorite toy puppies and hadn't paid much attention to the other kids, who'd made up games with rules that Abby hadn't been able to understand.

But in first grade, she'd gotten Amigo, and kids in her class had started paying a lot more attention to her. Mostly they had asked about Amigo, which had been Abby's favorite thing to talk about anyway.

Miriam had been one of those kids. She'd told Abby that she wanted a dog, but she couldn't have one because her father was allergic. Because Amigo was a service dog, other people weren't supposed to touch him or distract him while he was on the job. But Abby had made an exception for Miriam and said that she could pet Amigo whenever she wanted.

Abby had been a little worried that when she stopped bringing Amigo to class, she and Miriam would stop being friends. But so far, Miriam seemed to like hanging out with Abby even when Amigo wasn't around.

"It was a long report, but it was interesting,"

Miriam continued. "I didn't realize the Iditarod was such a difficult race. I can't imagine spending eight whole days out in the Alaskan wilderness."

"I know, right?" said Abby. "And I was surprised by how much the dogs have to eat—more than ten thousand calories per day! That's the equivalent of twenty-four Big Macs."

There was so much information that Abby hadn't been able to include in her report, and she wanted to share it with Miriam. After a few minutes, though, she stopped herself and let Miriam talk. That was something she'd had to learn on her own. Amigo was a smart dog, but even he didn't have an alert for when she was oversharing.

Today, Miriam had something on her mind that seemed to be even more important than dogs. "My brother got home from the army this weekend," she said as they filled their lunch trays and sat at their favorite table under the food pyramid mural the class had painted.

"My dad used to be in the army," said Abby, deconstructing the cafeteria's turkey sandwich into separate piles of bread, meat, cheese, and tomato so she could eat each ingredient separately. "But it was a long time ago, so I don't really remember. Natalie remembers it better." Natalie was two years older than Abby. Their younger sisters, Emily and Grace, were nine-year-old twins.

"It's weird because Caleb's been gone for three whole years," said Miriam, using her right hand to unwrap the straw from her box of apple juice and pierce the foil top with it. Miriam had cerebral palsy, a condition that weakened the muscles of her body, especially on the left side. She had some trouble lifting the juice box from the tray to her mouth, but Abby didn't offer to help. Miriam got annoyed when people tried to do things for her if she could do them herself.

"He's only come back for Hanukkah twice that whole time, and once for a week when our grandma died," Miriam continued, taking a sip of juice. "But now he's back for good."

"Are you glad to have him at home again?" asked Abby. When Emily and Grace had been adopted into the family three years ago, Abby had not been thrilled about suddenly having two new sisters who were nearly her own age—and who were often quite loud and used up all the hot water in the shower. But now she could hardly imagine life without them.

"I thought I would be," said Miriam. "But he's so different than I remember. He spends most of his time listening to music alone in his room. He doesn't even want to hang out with his old friends from high school, never mind me. I feel like I'm practically invisible to him."

Abby tried to think of reasons Miriam's brother might be acting that way. She had only met Caleb a few times, but she remembered him as being loud and friendly and liking basketball.

"Maybe he's sick," she said. "Or maybe he's still tired from traveling. I looked at Kuwait on the map, and it's really far away." Abby always felt tired and cranky after she had to take a long trip.

"Maybe," said Miriam. She took a few bites of her sandwich and then sighed and pushed her tray away.

"Do you want that?" asked Abby, pointing to the untouched brownie on Miriam's plate. Miriam shook her head, so Abby took the brownie and ate it so it wouldn't go to waste.

It sounded like Miriam had finished talking about her brother for now, so Abby started telling her the rest of what she had learned about sled dogs.

When she got home from school a few hours later, Abby dropped her backpack near the door and headed straight for the fleecy dog bed in the living room where Amigo liked to nap.

Abby's family ran an animal rescue called Second Chance Ranch, and it was Abby's job to help take care of all the dogs after school. Right now, the ranch had seven adult dogs and six puppies to look after. But no matter how busy she was, Abby always took Amigo for a walk first thing after she got home. She was a little surprised that he hadn't greeted her at the door with his leash in his mouth, like he often did.

Abby stopped in her tracks when she got to the living room and saw Amigo's empty bed. There was no trace of him except for the long golden hairs clinging to the white sheepskin fabric.

Abby hurried to the kennel room at the back of the house, in case he was there. The room was empty because all the dogs were outside in their runs for the afternoon. Abby hurried out the back door and peered into each chain-link pen. She counted each of the ranch's other dogs, including Cocoa the cocker spaniel with her six puppies. But there was no Amigo.

Abby looked upstairs in her bedroom, in her sisters' and parents' rooms, and in each of the bathrooms. She searched the basement and the attic, even though Amigo never went in those places.

After that, she had nowhere else to look. Amigo was gone!

Chapter Two

Panic rose in Abby's throat, making her feel like she was underwater and drowning. Could Amigo have gotten outside by accident? What if he'd been hit by a car, or someone had dognapped him?

She ran out to the big barn where the ranch's horses, goats, and other farm animals lived. There was no sign of Amigo, but Abby found her father and Marco, their fourteen-year-old neighbor who helped out around the ranch. They were replacing some worn-out boards in one of the horse stalls.

Abby couldn't think clearly enough to speak. Instead, she ran over to where her father was working. Just then he swung around with the board he was holding and knocked Abby to the ground.

"Abby!" he cried, dropping the board and kneeling in front of her. "You came out of nowhere! Are you alright?"

Abby gasped for breath, lying on the floor of the stall. But it wasn't just getting hit with the board that had knocked the wind out of her. It felt like all of her language was dissolving, and she could only think in pictures.

She saw Amigo's empty bed, the empty house.

She clenched her hand into a fist and bit down until she tasted blood.

"It's okay, sweetheart. Just calm down and take deep breaths," said her father, gently pulling her hand out of her mouth and helping her up. He held her by each shoulder. "Remember square breathing? Breath in—one, two, three. Hold—one, two, three. Out—one, two, three."

Abby tried to focus on her father's voice, inhaling, holding her breath, and then exhaling in an even pattern. She pictured a square in her head and each breath moving from one side of the square to the next. After five or six breaths, she was finally able to speak.

"Amigo," she said. "I can't find him!"

"Didn't you see the note I left on the refrigerator door?" asked her dad.

She shook her head. She had been so focused on looking for Amigo that she probably wouldn't have noticed if Natalie's fashion-obsessed friend Darcy had snuck in and redecorated their entire house.

"I took Amigo to the vet clinic this morning, not too long after you left for school," Mr. Ramirez said. "I noticed that he was panting hard and seemed unsteady on his legs. Your mom adjusted the dose of his heart medicine and gave him some IV fluids. He's still resting at the animal hospital."

"I want to see him now!" said Abby, still so upset that she forgot to ask nicely.

Her father looked around at the half-nailed boards and tools scattered around the stall.

"I can finish up this job myself," Marco said to Mr. Ramirez. Abby had forgotten he was even there.

"You sure about that?" Mr. Ramirez replied.

Marco nodded. He normally joked and teased, but now his face was serious. "I hope Amigo's okay," he said to Abby.

"I hope so too." Abby turned and ran to the car. She was already buckled in by the time Mr. Ramirez got there.

Ten minutes later, Abby burst through the double doors of the waiting room at Sugarberry Animal Hospital. A woman with a cat carrier and a couple of kids with a ferret on a leash looked up at her.

Abby ran up to the reception desk where her mom's assistant, Tina, was on the phone. Abby bounced up and down on her heels while Tina finished setting up an appointment for a new client. The second she hung up, Abby said, "My dog, Amigo, is here. Do you know where he is?"

"I sure do," said Tina, getting to her feet and stepping around her desk to lead Abby to a small office at the back of the building. Amigo was lying curled up in a big basket, with a clear tube running from his foreleg to a nearly empty IV bag.

He let out a little *woof* of joy when he saw Abby. She dropped down to her knees and hugged him, pressing her cheek against the silky fur of his neck.

"He's looking more perky than he did this morning," said Tina. "I'll go get your mom so she can check up on him."

A moment later, Tina returned with Abby's mom, who sat down on the floor with Abby and Amigo. "I'm so sorry you came home to find Amigo missing," she said. "Your dad told me you were really worried."

Abby nodded. "I thought Amigo might be . . . you know, *gone*." Abby couldn't quite bring herself to say what she really meant.

"No, I think Amigo's going to be with us for a while yet," Mrs. Ramirez said. She put a comforting hand on Abby's back.

Abby knew that if she were Natalie or Emily or Grace, her mom would have hugged her. But Abby didn't like to be hugged. To her, it felt too much like being crushed. Abby leaned up against her mother instead.

"Can Amigo go home now?" she asked.

Mrs. Ramirez put her stethoscope to her ears and listened to Amigo's heart.

"I think he's good to go," she said. She took out Amigo's IV and taped a piece of gauze over his leg. There was a little bare patch where his fur had been shaved.

Abby clipped Amigo's leash to his collar and led him slowly back to the car. Mr. Ramirez helped lift him into the back. When they got home, Abby asked Amigo if he wanted to go for a walk. But he just wagged his tail politely and then went to the living room to lie down on his bed. Abby brought him his favorite sheep toy and his red gummy bone, but Amigo just wanted to sleep.

Abby kept a close eye on him for the rest of the afternoon, running back to the den to check on him as she did her chores. Normally, Abby looked forward to giving all of the dogs some attention each day, but now she walked the dogs, fed them, and cleaned their kennels on autopilot. Even Cocoa and her puppies, which were getting cuter and more active by the day, couldn't distract Abby for long. At dinner, Abby insisted that Amigo lie next to her chair at the table, even though he wasn't normally allowed.

Some evenings, the family did an activity together after dinner, like watching a movie or playing a board game. But tonight, everyone was doing their own thing. Her parents sat at the table by the window, playing cards. Natalie was in the big armchair on her laptop, updating the ranch's blog. Grace sat cross-legged in front of the TV, playing a video game, and Emily was curled up on the couch, reading.

Amigo had gone back to his bed again, and Abby decided that a good grooming might make him feel better. She was right—as soon as he saw the brush, he sat up. His tail waved gently from side to side on the carpet as Abby ran the brush again and again through his silky, slightly wavy fur.

Abby wondered how many times she had brushed Amigo like this before. Hundreds of times. Maybe thousands. She remembered the first time she had set eyes on Amigo in the service-dog training center, when she was just six years old.

"Who's that?" Abby had asked when she'd seen

the solemn-looking golden retriever sitting in the corner, apart from the other dogs.

The trainer had told Abby that Amigo had spent the last few years as a service dog for a little boy with a rare disease. The boy had died, and his family had brought Amigo back to the training center because they were too sad to keep him.

The service-dog trainer had introduced Abby and her parents to four different dogs that had passed their public access test and were ready to be placed in a permanent home. There had been two Labradors, a corgi, and a standard poodle. They had all been so happy and obedient, with wagging tails and panting mouths that seemed to say, "Pick me, pick me!"

Abby had wished she could take all of them home. But for some reason, it was Amigo she chose, even though he was just sitting there, apart from the other dogs, watching her with those serious brown eyes. It was like he was speaking to her with his gaze, telling her that he needed another child to look after. And Abby needed him too.

That had been four years ago. Abby didn't really like to think about the time before she got Amigo, because she had been so confused and upset so much of the time. She remembered crying a lot and not being able to find the words to tell people what she wanted.

Sometimes back then, she would just lie on the floor and cover her ears and yell if anyone tried to touch her. Her family had called those "meltdowns," and they had happened almost every day, especially when Abby had started kindergarten but could only say a few words. She still remembered the day she had been sent home early for biting the ankle of a kid who kept putting his feet all over her mat at rest time.

Abby wasn't sure exactly how Amigo had helped her find the words, because he couldn't speak himself. But somehow, he had. Just having him around seemed to help her brain settle down enough to make her thoughts and feelings and speech connect to each other. Now Abby could read even faster than Natalie, and her sisters often teased her about all the big words she used.

Abby set down the brush and stroked Amigo's head. Her hands lingered on the short gray hairs around his muzzle. She saw Amigo every day, but somehow she hadn't really noticed them before. Now, even more than the heart medicine Abby had to give him every morning, the gray hairs seemed like unavoidable proof that Amigo was getting old.

The thing was, usually whenever Abby tried to picture the future, Amigo was with her. She could imagine him wagging his tail at her high school graduation, carrying the ring down the aisle for her when she got married, and going with her on a fieldwork assignment into the wilderness when she became a famous scientist.

But lately, Abby couldn't imagine these things at all, because she knew they weren't real. Amigo wouldn't be with her forever, and just the thought of that made her feel like having the worst meltdown of her life. So she tried not to think about it at all.

Instead, she went to the kitchen and came back with a handful of Amigo's favorite jerky treats. When Abby first got Amigo, his trainer had recommended that Abby not teach him a lot of new tricks. Instead, she'd worked to reinforce the commands he had already learned: nudging her hand if she started to get anxious, leading her to her backpack if she started to leave it behind, and moving to stand between her and strangers in crowded situations.

But now that Amigo was mostly retired, Abby had started to teach him some tricks just for fun. He had already learned to shake hands with visitors who came to the ranch on open-house days. Now, Abby decided to teach him a trick she'd seen in an online video.

She took three red plastic cups left over from their summer barbecue and turned them upside down. She put a piece of jerky underneath one, making sure Amigo could see it, and then lined up the cups.

"Find it!" said Abby.

Amigo reached out with his nose and snuffled at the cup with the hidden jerky.

"Good find," said Abby, lifting the cup so he could have the treat.

Abby did the same thing again but slowly swirled the cups around before lining them up. Amigo kept his eye on the cup with the jerky. When she stopped, he reached out to sniff the right one.

Next, Abby took a rainbow-colored ball and put it under one of the cups, along with a treat. She mixed them up and said, "Find it!"

Once again, Amigo reached out his nose to poke at the cup that hid the treat.

Now Abby tried it with just the ball. Amigo still picked the right cup, and Abby gave him a piece of jerky as a reward.

Just like that, Amigo had learned a new trick. He'd learned it even faster than the border collie in the video, and border collies were supposed to be one of the smartest dog breeds.

Playing with Amigo made Abby feel better. He couldn't be that sick if he was still so clever. But Abby thought that if she ever did become a famous scientist, the first thing she'd do would be to invent a pill that made dogs live as long as people did.

Chapter Three

"Wait!" Abby cried, running after the school bus. But it was too late. The bus was already pulling away down the winding country road and turning the corner, out of sight. And with it, Abby's backpack, her homework, and her schoolbooks.

Abby sighed. Most people used the dog-ate-my-homework excuse to avoid turning it in. Abby's dog had reminded her not to forget her homework!

She trudged up the ranch's long driveway and was surprised to see her father in the parking area near the barn, talking to a muscular man covered in tattoos. Between them was a large animal crate with solid plastic sides.

Abby edged closer so she could hear what they were saying but not so close that the man would notice her. She didn't like meeting strangers, and this guy didn't look very friendly.

". . . bought this dog as a little anti-theft policy for my car lot, but she's afraid of her own shadow. No good to me at all."

Abby ducked behind an apple tree in the yard and waited while her father had the man sign some paperwork. As the man was getting in his car to leave,

Abby stepped out from behind the tree and called out to him, "Hey! What's her name?"

It bothered Abby when animals came to the farm and no one knew their names. Her sisters liked picking new names, but Abby thought it was only fair for an animal to have one name in its life. She wouldn't have been very happy if everyone had suddenly started calling her Maria or Elizabeth or something.

The man looked surprised. "Guy who sold her to me said it was 'Destiny,'" he replied in a gruff voice. "Not her destiny to be a guard dog, that's for sure." He slammed his car door and drove away, leaving the crate in the middle of the driveway beside Mr. Ramirez.

Abby hurried over and kneeled down to peer into the crate. The inside was so dark that Abby could only see the shine of eyes and the dull gleam of a black nose.

She started to reach for the crate but froze when her father yelled, "Stop!" Abby looked up at him. "You remember the rule," he said in a softer voice. "We never approach a new dog in its crate, because it might feel cornered and threatened. We'll let her out into one of the runs so she can come to us when she's ready."

Mr. Ramirez walked around to the side of the crate and lifted it by the handle on the top. A low growl came from within. Abby could tell the crate was heavy by the way her father moved across the yard with slow, lurching steps.

She opened the gate to one of the empty dog runs—a narrow, grassy pen enclosed by a chain-link fence. Her father set down the crate inside, opened the door, and then backed out of the pen, closing the gate behind him.

He and Abby both watched to see what would happen.

First, a long muzzle poked out and sniffed at the grass, followed by a pair of pointed black-tipped ears and one big golden-brown paw, then another. Soon,

the entire dog was out of the crate, slinking around the edge of the pen with her nose to the ground.

Destiny was a beautiful German shepherd. Her fur was a tawny golden color, thicker and coarser than Amigo's, with a black saddle-shaped marking on her back. She had a black muzzle and black-tipped ears that stood up alertly, swiveling around to take in the many sounds of the ranch, from the barks of other dogs to the distant whinnies of the horses in the pasture to the drone of the lawnmower Marco was using in the backyard.

Abby knew that German shepherds were often used for protection. But this one looked more like she needed protecting. Destiny made a cautious circuit of her pen and then returned to her crate only to find that the wind had swung the door closed. Now she cowered nearly flat on the ground, her tail tucked between her legs. A high-pitched whine rose in the back of her throat.

Abby wanted to approach the dog and comfort her, but she could tell from the dog's tense body language that she might bite.

Abby's dad had taught her that dogs never bite for no reason. You couldn't always know the reason, but you could nearly always see the signs. Growling, bared teeth, and raised hackles on the back of a dog's neck were only the most obvious clues. Even submissive body language like ducking away, rolling over, or licking and yawning could mean that a dog might bite from fear.

Cowering by her crate, Destiny seemed as overwhelmed as Abby had felt on her first day of school. Suddenly, Abby wondered if Amigo might be able to help Destiny like he'd helped her.

She ran into the living room and found Amigo, who was grooming his toy sheep. It was funny—he never chewed on his soft toys or pulled out their stuffing. He only licked them as if he were a mother cat giving her kittens a bath.

"I've got a job for you, buddy!" said Abby, and Amigo got up stiffly but eagerly to his feet.

She brought him outside and led him into the empty dog run next to Destiny's. Amigo walked over and pressed his nose up against the fence. His tail wagged, and he let out a friendly *woof*.

Destiny sniffed cautiously in his direction but didn't move from where she was cowered against the closed door of her crate.

Amigo flopped down onto the grass and began chewing on an old tennis ball. Destiny kept a close eye on him. A few minutes later, she sank slowly to her haunches and inched her front legs forward until she was lying down too.

"Look, Amigo's helping her relax," said Abby. "She doesn't trust us yet, but she'll trust another dog telling her it's safe here."

"I can see," said Mr. Ramirez. "That was smart thinking."

The other dogs were starting to bark and get restless because it was their dinner time. Abby went into the kennel and filled each dog's bowl with kibble or canned food, along with any medicine or supplements.

When Abby got to Amigo's dish, she soaked his dry food with just enough water to moisten it but not enough to make it soggy. She crushed up one of his heart pills in the pill crusher and mixed the powder with canned turkey-flavored dog food—Amigo's favorite.

"What should I give Destiny?" she asked her dad, grabbing an extra dish from the supply closet.

"I'd say two cups of adult dog kibble to start with and half a can of wet food," he said.

Abby went over and scooped out the food from the correct bag. It was a huge hundred-pound sack, nearly as tall as Abby, because they went through so much of the stuff. Luckily, the ranch got a special nonprofit discount at the local feed store.

Abby carried Amigo's supper out to his pen, but her father insisted on taking Destiny's dish.

"I don't want you going in there until we know if she's safe to handle," he said.

When he entered Destiny's pen, she jumped to her feet and loped to the far end, watching him warily. The second he shut the gate and was outside again,

Destiny rushed forward and gobbled up the food as if she'd never eaten in her life. It made Abby sad and somehow angry to see, because it was clear that at some point, Destiny had gone hungry.

Abby went into Amigo's pen and set down his supper. He sat patiently, waiting until she told him, "Okay!"

She was glad to see that he started eating right away, although not as eagerly as Destiny. He'd been a little picky about his food lately, probably because of the pills. Maybe being outside in the fresh air was stimulating his appetite.

The late-spring sunshine felt warm on Abby's shoulders. "It's so nice out," she said to her dad. "Do you think it's okay to leave Amigo out here with Destiny for the night?"

Her father agreed, and Abby helped bring the other dogs into the kennel for the night. Some of the rescue dogs were great escape artists, and others liked to pick fights, so they all got shut into their own crates for the night.

Sometimes people thought putting a dog in a crate was mean, but Abby knew that dogs actually felt safer in familiar enclosed spaces, like the caves their ancestors might have slept in. *If* they were comfortable with their environment, anyway. Destiny was still so fearful that she would probably have felt trapped. Hopefully Amigo's presence would help her feel safe.

A savory aroma wafting from the kitchen altered Abby to the fact that her own dinner was probably almost ready. When she had finished with the dogs, she went into the kitchen and found Natalie putting a garnish of lime on some plates of shrimp tacos coated with an alarmingly heavy dusting of cayenne pepper.

"Don't worry. Yours is chicken, and it's separate," she said as she saw Abby's worried look.

"Thanks," Abby said, glad that Natalie had remembered she didn't like seafood or a lot of spice.

She helped Natalie set the table, and by the time Abby had put the last fork and knife on the last napkin, the rest of the family had found their way to the kitchen.

A few minutes later, Abby was happily biting into her non-spicy chicken taco when Natalie said, "I need to go shopping for a new bathing suit. There's a sale at the mall. Can we go this weekend?"

"Sure," said Mrs. Ramirez. "I need to get a new sun hat myself."

"I could use a new suit too," said Emily. "I grew a lot this year."

"Me too," said Grace. "Actually, I grew a quarter-inch more than Emily did. We measured against the doorframe this morning. I also need some new soccer shorts because my white ones got totally grass-stained when I fell on the field this weekend. We played Sassafras Springs, and those kids are such cheaters. Their star forward tripped me on purpose, I'm sure of it." Grace held up her arm to show a skinned elbow.

"That's not fair!" said Emily, jumping to her sister's defense. "You should tell your coach."

"Nah, I don't want to be a tattletale. Besides, I got her back by loosening the top of her water bottle. She got a cold shower instead of a drink!" Grace snickered with glee, and the girls' parents shook their heads. They were always trying to talk Grace out of her pranks, but they never had any luck.

"Wait a minute, how come you all need new bathing suits now?" asked Abby, who had tried her hardest to not interrupt until Grace had finished telling about her soccer game. "It's not summer yet, and we don't even have a pool."

"Have you forgotten what we do every year during summer vacation?" Natalie asked. "School gets out in three weeks, and I don't want to wait too long and end up with an ugly bathing suit covered in neon flowers because that's all that's left at the store."

Abby dropped her fork onto her plate with a clatter. She had completely forgotten about her family's yearly vacation. It was worse than having to go to school. It was worse than being trapped in a movie theater and getting squished up against strangers who loudly slurped their drinks. It was maybe even worse than going to the dentist to have a cavity filled.

Every summer, her family spent a week at the beach.

Chapter Four

Whenever Abby wanted to be alone, she retreated to what she called her Cave of Solitude. It was actually a junior camping tent in sky blue, Abby's favorite color. The Cave of Solitude took up a whole corner of Abby's room, but for her it was an extra layer of privacy in the often busy and noisy Ramirez household. Nobody was allowed to bother her when she was in it, except in an emergency.

Inside was a down sleeping bag and a weighted blanket that she could wrap herself in like a cocoon. She also had an iPod filled with her favorite music, a set of aromatherapy oils, some books, and a notebook for journaling. Her school's guidance counselor, LeeAnn, had suggested that Abby try journaling to put her thoughts and feelings into words.

Now Abby zipped herself into the Cave of Solitude, opened her notebook, and poised her pen over a blank page.

Reasons I hate the beach, she wrote. She thought for a moment, and then started writing so quickly that her handwriting got messy and hard to read.

1. *Seagulls*
2. *Hot sand like lava under my feet*
3. *Gross public restrooms*

4. *Smearing cold glops of sunscreen over my body*
5. *The smell of decaying fish*
6. *Screaming babies who also hate the beach*
7. *Drinks don't stay cold*
8. *The feel of seaweed wrapping around my leg*
9. *The constant threat of jellyfish*
10. *Seagulls*

Abby realized she had written seagulls twice, but that only emphasized how much she didn't like them. Their cries were deafening, they were giant aerial poop bombs, and they gathered in huge, creepy flocks whenever you had something to eat.

Abby had reached the end of the page, and she could have gone on, but she had written enough to remind herself why she was dreading the upcoming vacation. Or at least the part where they went to the beach. She actually liked the condo her family rented every year and the cool museums, aquariums, and restaurants they always went to.

But every summer, Abby stayed behind in the clean, safe, air-conditioned living room to read or watch movies while everyone else went to the beach— except one of her parents always stayed with her, and Abby felt bad for making them miss out. Her parents worked so hard and took vacations so rarely.

Abby wanted to be a good sport and go to the beach with the rest of her family; it was just so overwhelming. And dogs weren't allowed on public beaches, so she couldn't bring Amigo.

The last time she'd gone to the beach with everyone, when she was seven, she'd ended up being stung by a dead jellyfish, accidentally swallowing a mouthful of disgusting seawater, and getting hit upside the head with a beach ball some kid had thrown at her—and then finally having a huge meltdown on the hot, hot sand. After that, Abby just hadn't been able to bring herself to go back.

Well, that settled it. Abby closed her notebook and emerged from the Cave of Solitude. Maybe when her sisters went to the mall to buy bathing suits, Abby could go along and get some new books to read while everyone else was at the beach.

At school the next day, Abby got back her graded report on sled dogs. Her grade was an A-. Mr. Timothy had written, *Well researched and good job staying on topic. Sled dogs are amazing animals! Try to remember to look up at the class instead of just reading from your notes.*

For science that day, the class got to take a mini field trip into the woods behind the school for a scavenger hunt. Some items, like a pinecone and a piece of quartz, they could put in their nature boxes. Others, like a wildflower and an anthill, were marked "Do Not Disturb," which meant they were only supposed to bring the rest of the class to see them.

"Do you think this is quartz?" asked Abby, fishing into a stream. She walked the few feet to the trail where Miriam was studying a plant and held up a smooth white pebble for her to inspect.

"I'm not sure," said Miriam, glancing at it briefly. "Maybe."

That was odd, because Miriam had a huge collection of rocks and gemstones at home. If anyone in their class could identify a piece of quartz, it was her.

Then Abby realized that Miriam had hardly said a word all afternoon. The whole way into the woods, Abby had told Miriam about all her research on German shepherd dogs. Even Abby felt like she was talking too much, but Miriam hadn't even stopped her by saying, "TMI, Abby Labrador!," like she usually did when Abby's explanations started to become overkill.

"Abby Labrador" was Miriam's nickname for Abby, which Abby liked even though she thought that if she were a dog, she'd be an Airedale terrier because they were independent and had light-brown fur that reminded Abby of her own hair.

Abby knew that when an animal—or in Miriam's case, a person—started acting much differently than usual, it often meant something was wrong.

"Is everything okay?" she asked Miriam, who was

steering her wheelchair toward a glade up ahead. They were on the hunt for a puffball mushroom. "You're unusually quiet today."

"Well," Miriam said, "last night my brother had a big argument with my parents. I don't even know what it was about. But I heard him yelling, and then he left and didn't come back until this morning. I asked him what was wrong, but he just said not to worry about it. And then he asked if I wanted to watch my favorite Tinkerbell DVD. Yeah, my favorite when I was *six*! I don't think he realizes that I'm not a little kid anymore."

Abby didn't know how to reply. She wasn't like Natalie, who always had advice for people. "Maybe you should tell him what movies you like to watch now," she said finally. "Then you won't have to watch dumb ones."

"Yeah, that's a good point," said Miriam, and Abby felt a little like Amigo looked when he managed to jump up and catch a ball in midair. Maybe she wasn't completely hopeless when it came to helping people with their problems after all.

"Hey, over there!" said Miriam, pointing to a glittering chunk of rock on the bank of a bend in the stream. "That's *definitely* quartz."

"Will you look at that?" Mr. Ramirez said later that afternoon, pausing in the kennel doorway as he led Bonnie the boxer inside to have her nails clipped.

Abby looked up from the freshly washed dog bedding she was hanging on the line to dry and saw that Amigo and Destiny were playing a game with the tennis ball Amigo had found, passing it back and forth under a gap in the fence.

Abby smiled and walked over to watch them—and maybe join their game. But when Destiny noticed Abby approaching, she dropped the tennis ball and took a few wary steps back.

"Careful, Abby," Mr. Ramirez warned as she approached the pen. "I don't want you going in there with her yet."

Abby visited with Amigo instead and gave him a good scratch behind the ears. Then he rolled onto his back with his paws in the air. Abby gave him a belly rub, watching Destiny from the corner of her eye.

Just as she suspected, Destiny began to inch closer as she saw how much Amigo was enjoying the attention. Still talking to Amigo, Abby reached out one hand and held it flat against the chain-link fence. A minute later, she felt Destiny lick her open palm. Her fringed black-and-tan tail had untucked itself from its clamped-down position and was wagging cautiously.

Abby looked up at her dad, who was still watching. "Now can I try going into her pen?" she asked.

"Okay," her dad said. "But be careful and watch her body language. If she growls, I want you out of there."

Moving almost in slow motion, Abby entered Destiny's pen and sat down in the grass. She didn't make eye contact with Destiny but grabbed the tennis ball from where Destiny had dropped it and started tossing it from hand to hand.

After a few minutes, Abby felt Destiny approach. She sat down about six feet away with her ears perked alertly in Abby's direction.

Abby rolled the ball across the ground toward Destiny. She trapped the ball with her paws, and then picked it up in her strong jaws. Abby couldn't help noticing how big and sharp her teeth were. She could have crushed the tennis ball in one chomp if she wanted to. Instead, Destiny stood up and dropped the now slightly soggy ball into Abby's lap.

Abby took the ball and threw it across the pen for Destiny to fetch. But Destiny didn't follow the ball. She was still looking at Abby, and suddenly, she lay down and rested her head on Abby's knee with a big sigh.

"See? It's not so scary here, is it?" Abby said. She scratched Destiny's neck around her worn blue collar. It was a good, neutral place to pet a dog you didn't

know, unlike trying to touch its head or belly right away, which might be seen as a threat.

Destiny thumped her tail on the ground and began to pant happily, like Amigo did when he was relaxing and enjoying her attention.

"Remarkable," her dad said. "I don't know how you do it, Abby." He took Bonnie inside and then came back outside to Destiny's pen. But when he started to open the gate, Destiny leaped up as if she'd been zapped with a shock collar. She backed up until she bumped into the back wall of her pen, letting out shrill, loud barks that made Abby's ears ring.

Mr. Ramirez motioned for Abby to leave the pen.

"I just don't know about that dog," he said, shaking his head. "She might be better off at a shelter that can do advanced rehab work for dogs with behavioral problems."

"But she didn't growl or bite," Abby said, looking at Destiny, who was still cowering at the far end of the pen. "She's not aggressive; she's just scared."

"No, she didn't growl," Mr. Ramirez said. "But she's so unpredictable that I wouldn't feel comfortable letting her be adopted."

Abby thought hard. She didn't think Destiny should be sent away just when she'd started to trust people—or at least, to trust Abby.

"Can we let Destiny be an inside dog with Amigo for a while?" asked Abby. "I think that being around him helps her. And she'll get over her fear of us more quickly if she's around us more."

Mr. Ramirez looked doubtful. "You know we can't let all the rescued animals have the run of the house. There'd be no room for us!" He often had this conversation with Emily, who always wanted new kittens and cats to sleep in her room.

"I don't want to let *all* the dogs in," said Abby. "Just Destiny."

"Well, all right," her dad said reluctantly. "We can try it for a few days and see how it goes."

"Great!" Abby grabbed a leash from the kennel before her dad could change his mind. Destiny trotted over right away when Abby called her name. She even sat on command while Abby clipped the leash to her collar. And she only barked once when Abby led her past Mr. Ramirez and into the house.

Chapter Five

A week later, Destiny had adjusted pretty well to life as an inside dog. She still tried to hide behind furniture when Mr. Ramirez came into the room, but she wasn't nearly as skittish around Mrs. Ramirez or Abby's sisters. Destiny seemed to only be afraid of men.

Well, that plus a long list of other things, including vacuum cleaners, washing machines, fans, piles of laundry, umbrellas, ringing phones, people wearing hats, and Grace's victory dance when she moved up to a new level in her video game.

Oh, and cheese. Abby had discovered that one when she'd gone to give Amigo his bedtime treat. It was only fair for Destiny to get one, too, but she'd turned up her nose at Amigo's favorite jerky strips. She also wasn't interested in the bone-shaped treats from the big box in the kennel. A lot of dogs liked cheese, so Abby had unwrapped a slice of cheddar from the fridge and offered half of it to Destiny.

When Destiny had sniffed the cheese, her eyes had bugged out, and she'd backed away so fast that she'd crashed into the kitchen counter.

Abby had no idea how a dog could become afraid of cheese—but out of any dog Abby had met, she wasn't surprised that it was Destiny who had that phobia. Even though she was a big, strong German shepherd, Destiny seemed to see herself as a tiny Chihuahua. Actually, that wasn't fair—the ranch's rescued Chihuahua, Estrella, strutted around like she owned the place. Destiny was more like a frightened bunny rabbit. Anyway, cheese was definitely out as a reward. But it turned out that Destiny liked baby carrots even better than any rabbit would, so those were her new bedtime snack.

Now Abby grabbed two leashes so she could take Destiny and Amigo out together. When Destiny saw that Amigo was unfazed by horses, chickens, tractors, lawnmowers, and all the other stuff they ran into on the ranch, she stayed much calmer than when Abby had taken her out alone.

"Who's ready for a walk?" said Abby, entering the living room where Amigo was napping on his bed and Destiny was chewing on a Nylabone toy.

Amigo raised his head briefly, and then flopped back onto his side with a sigh. His breaths grew deep and heavy; he was practically snoring.

"I get it, I get it," said Abby. "You don't have to be so dramatic."

Clearly, Amigo wasn't in the mood for a walk, but Destiny was practically dancing with anticipation.

"Looks like it's just you and me, girl," Abby said, clipping the leash to Destiny's collar. She'd found a new collar for Destiny in their donation bin of supplies. Aside from being shabby, Destiny's old one had probably been connected with a lot of unpleasant memories.

Destiny nearly dragged Abby through the house and out the door. It was obvious that no one had worked on her leash manners recently—if ever.

Outside, Abby saw Emily playing with some kittens on the lawn. She took a shorter hold on Destiny's leash and headed over, figuring it was a good opportunity to introduce Destiny to something new.

About ten feet away, Destiny suddenly saw where they were headed and refused to walk any farther. She ducked behind Abby and peered out suspiciously from behind her back.

"Really?" said Abby. "You're afraid of *kittens*?"

Two of the kittens were play-fighting, and they rolled closer and closer to Destiny. She kept her paws rooted to the spot but slowly stretched her neck out longer and longer until she almost looked like a giraffe.

The kittens noticed Destiny and froze with their arms wrapped around each other, their blue eyes wide and startled. One of the kittens streaked back over to Emily like a fuzzy rocket. But the other—a gray-and-black tabby—rolled playfully in the grass. Destiny took one step forward and gave the kitten a wary poke with her nose. The friendly tabby rubbed its tiny head against hers.

Destiny poked the kitten again, just a little too hard. Startled, the kitten hissed and swiped at Destiny's nose with its tiny claws. Destiny let out a shrill bark and snapped at the kitten.

"No, Destiny!" Abby scolded, pulling on the leash to drag Destiny back.

Emily rushed over and scooped up the frightened kitten, clutching it to her chest.

"You keep that dog away from my cats, Abby!" she yelled. Her cheeks were flushed, and her eyes blazed. Abby had seen Grace that mad before, but never Emily. Abby tightened up on Destiny's leash and quickly brought her inside.

Had Abby's dad been right? Did Destiny need the help of a professional dog trainer? Abby had worked with puppies and even adult dogs that had no training before, but never one as unpredictable as Destiny.

Still, Destiny hadn't actually hurt the kitten. And what if Abby's parents had given up on *her* when she was younger and more easily upset, instead of helping her work through it?

Well, Abby wasn't going to give up on Destiny. She marched up to her room, turned on her computer, and typed "training a dog with behavior problems" into the search engine.

Right away, tons of articles and videos popped

up. Abby was in her element. If there was a way to help Destiny, Abby would find it.

"Okay, Marco, now give her the carrot," said Abby. Destiny had just done a perfect "sit-stay" command. But Abby wasn't really working on Destiny's obedience—although that needed some brushing up too. She was working on Abby's fear of men.

Abby had found a lot of dog-training tips online— some good, some not so good. Cesar Millan, who had a show called *The Dog Whisperer*, had a lot of advice on working with fearful dogs. One thing he mentioned was that dogs were sometimes too smart for their own good and made associations too easily. If Destiny had been treated badly by a male owner in the past, she might generalize that to *all* men. The only way to help her get over that fear was to create new, positive experiences.

So Abby had enlisted Marco's help for this session. It was just like training Abby would do with any dog—except that whenever Destiny earned a reward, she had to take it from Marco, not Abby.

When Destiny had first realized this, she had looked at Abby like she'd been betrayed. Her expression had been so dramatic that Abby'd had to laugh. At first, Destiny had refused to take the carrot from

Marco. But as Abby kept working through her basic commands, Destiny had realized that if she wanted any treat at all, she would have to take it from Marco.

The first time, Destiny had snatched the carrot out of his hand like a ninja and then retreated halfway across the yard to eat it. But now, only half an hour later, she was eating the carrot right from Marco's hand—then licking it clean. Abby had never known a dog so motivated by vegetables before.

"See, I'm not such a bad guy, am I?" said Marco, giving Destiny a scratch behind the ears. "Maybe sometime you can come to my school and tell that to Elena Evans."

Abby giggled. She knew that Marco really wanted Elena Evans to be his girlfriend, but Elena didn't seem too interested so far. Abby decided not to tell Natalie, though. According to Emily, Natalie had a crush on Marco. Abby wasn't sure if that was true— Natalie didn't giggle or blush around Marco or do any of the stuff that people who had crushes were supposed to do. But Abby had never had a crush on anyone before, so she didn't know for sure if that was true or just a TV stereotype.

Later, Mr. Ramirez fed Destiny her supper and her bedtime treat. By the end of the week, Destiny had also met Marco's dad, Abby's uncle Robert, Grace's soccer coach, and the postal worker.

Destiny had been especially freaked out by the postal worker. She had even growled at him. Luckily, he was used to being less than popular among dogs. He had been more than willing to help out with Abby's training project once she told him about it, and he'd said he wished more owners would take the trouble to introduce their dogs to him properly. Once Destiny learned to associate the postal worker with carrots, he was practically her new best friend. Now she actually waited for him by the door every day.

Abby could hardly believe how quickly Destiny was making progress. She reminded Abby of the wild rabbits that often hid under their barn during a thunderstorm until it was safe to come out and graze on the lawn again. It upset Abby to imagine what Destiny must have gone through to make her so cautious in the first place. But just like Amigo had done for Abby, she'd soon show Destiny that there was no reason to be scared anymore.

The next day, Destiny got a break from her training while Abby spent the afternoon with Miriam at her house. They did some homework together, finished a puzzle of some puppies chasing butterflies that Miriam had started, and then decided to play Monopoly. They set up the game on the big table in the den downstairs, which was next to Caleb's room.

Miriam and Abby nearly always played Monopoly when they visited each other, and their games could get pretty competitive. Miriam let out a real wail of anguish when Abby landed on Park Place and snapped up the deed to accompany the Boardwalk neighborhood she already owned.

The door to Caleb's room burst open. He stood there with his clothes and hair rumpled and his eyes all squinty. "Will you two keep it down?" he said with an angry face and a voice that was nearly a yell. "Some people are trying to sleep around here!"

"Sorry," said Miriam in the little mouse voice she'd begun her book report with.

Abby didn't laugh now, either.

Caleb went back into his room and shut the door behind him. Actually, he slammed it.

"Who sleeps at two o'clock in the afternoon?" Abby whispered to Miriam. She was afraid to even talk in a regular voice.

"It seems like all he ever does is sleep now," said Miriam softly. "Unless he's using the gym equipment in the basement. Last night I woke up and heard him running on the treadmill at two in the morning!"

Abby pretended not to notice that Miriam looked like she was about to cry. They finished their Monopoly game, but it wasn't as much fun when they had to be so quiet.

Chapter Six

The next afternoon, Amigo was once again too tired to take a walk. Abby decided to walk Destiny into town, where there were lots of new sights and smells for her. Abby got the okay from her parents, along with their usual warnings about keeping an eye on the traffic and not talking to strangers. Since Sugarberry was a tiny town and the Ramirez family had lived there for Abby's whole life, there weren't all that many strangers to be found in the first place.

Downtown Sugarberry was about a mile from the ranch, and Abby was hot and thirsty by the time they reached the multifamily houses clustered at the edge of town. She decided to stop at the feed store for a soda—and a drink of water for Destiny. And Destiny could meet Mr. Jackson, the store owner.

Instead of passing through the busy center of town, she took a shortcut up a side street she didn't usually take. Destiny seemed reluctant to go down the street. Abby had to keep tugging her forward. Many of the houses on the road had boarded-up windows, and there was one big lot filled with old cars, its tall fence topped with rows of barbed wire.

Abby's steps slowed as she looked at all the broken-down cars. She remembered that the man who'd dropped off Destiny had said he owned a car lot. Could this be his property?

Destiny had stopped in her tracks and refused to take another step. Her whole body was trembling. Abby decided it would be better to turn around and go back through the center of town, but poor Destiny seemed too frightened to move at all.

"Come on, girl," Abby said, walking backward while making a coaxing gesture to show there was nothing to be afraid of. She accidentally kicked an empty glass bottle on the sidewalk and sent it spinning. It hit the barbed-wire fence with a resounding *clang!*

Abby stepped over to the fence to pick it up. She didn't like to see litter lying on the ground, and there was a recycling bin at the feed store. Just then, a howl split the air. Two massive black Dobermans hurtled out from the rusted-out body of a sedan and threw themselves at the fence.

Abby tripped and fell backward onto the sidewalk. The Dobermans kept leaping at the fence, which bulged and strained against their weight. Their jaws snapped, and the air was filled with the sound of their wild barking.

Destiny's leash slipped out of Abby's hand as she bolted away from the other dogs. Abby leaped to her feet and chased after Destiny. She grabbed the trailing end of Destiny's leash, stopping her just before

she ran in front of a huge pickup truck with spinning rims on its wheels.

Behind them, the Dobermans were still barking. Abby's heart was pounding so fast, it felt like a trapped animal in her chest. She didn't want a soda from the general store now—she just wanted to go home.

But Abby was still holding the glass bottle—somehow it hadn't broken. Sometimes Abby had trouble changing her plan once she had decided to do something, and now she felt like she just *had* to put that bottle in the recycling bin. The feed store was only a short distance away, and Abby decided she'd just sneak around back and put the bottle in the bin on the back porch without having to talk to anyone.

Unfortunately, Mr. Jackson was bringing a big box of empty egg cartons outside just as Abby was putting her bottle in with the others. She tried to encourage Destiny to hop down off the porch before he spotted her.

Too late. In his big, booming voice, Mr. Jackson waved to them and said, "Howdy, Abby! Didn't expect to see you around here today." He grunted as he set the box down and wiped his brow.

Abby stopped and turned around reluctantly. Mr. Jackson was over six feet tall and wide enough to block the steps leading off the porch. Plus, he liked to talk so he would be difficult to escape from.

"Hello, Mr. Jackson," Abby said, addressing a crack in the boards. Usually, Abby liked Mr. Jackson because he always gave Amigo a treat when they went to visit his store. But she also found him tiring to be around because he talked so loudly. And Abby didn't feel like talking to anyone right then.

"Call me Arnie," Mr. Jackson said. He always asked Abby and her sisters to call him Arnie. Abby preferred to call adults by their last name, so she always called him Mr. Jackson.

"And who's this?" he boomed. He reached out with his huge hand to pat Destiny's head, but she skittered back out of reach.

"Her name's Destiny," Abby said. She would have told Mr. Jackson that Destiny was rescued and Abby was training her, but the words seemed to swirl away out of reach. Abby felt her heart start to beat almost as fast as when the Dobermans were barking at her. Even though her mind knew she was safe, it was like her body was still on high alert.

Destiny looked from Abby to Mr. Jackson and back again. Her tail started to clamp, and her ears flattened back against her head with worry.

"Well now, I guess she's living the good life over at Second Chance Ranch," said Mr. Jackson. "Heck, I envy your critters. If I could pass myself off as a Saint Bernard, I might just try to take up residence myself!" He chuckled to himself.

Abby smiled weakly. She wanted to push past Mr. Jackson and go home, but she knew that would be rude.

"Oh, that reminds me!" he said, increasing the volume of his voice even more. "I've got a check for your parents to refund them for those bags of moldy rabbit feed. Again, I'm real sorry about that—won't be stocking that brand again, I can tell you."

He took out his wallet, removed a folded piece of paper, and thrust his hand out toward Abby. Startled by the sudden movement, she jumped back.

In the blink of an eye, Destiny lunged forward and grabbed Mr. Jackson's wrist. He bellowed like a startled bull then managed to pull his arm away.

Abby saw that Destiny's jaws had closed over the wide leather band of his watch. She caught a glimpse of its shattered crystal face.

Abby grabbed Destiny by the collar, jumped off the side of the porch, and ran as fast as she could away from the feed store. Destiny was only too happy to follow her.

"Whoa, Abby, what's wrong?" asked Emily as Abby came careening into the yard. The twins were both out with their ponies. Emily was grazing Bluebonnet on the lush grass of the lawn. Nearby, Grace was sitting bareback on Joker while she held his lead rope in one hand.

Abby stopped in her tracks and took up a tighter hold on Destiny, afraid the dog might bite at the horses like she had at Mr. Jackson. Abby was especially careful with Destiny around Emily, even though she had apologized for yelling at Abby about the kittens.

But to Abby's surprise, Destiny wagged her tail at Blue, her eyes bright. Blue, who was used to dogs around the ranch, tossed her head playfully. Destiny sank down into a frisky bow.

"Hey, look at her!" Emily said. "She's really making progress, isn't she?"

Abby shook her head. "I don't know about that," she said. "She bit Mr. Jackson just now."

"She *bit* him?" Emily asked, her blue eyes widening.

"What happened?" Grace asked, riding Joker closer—but not too close to Destiny, Abby noticed.

"Mr. Jackson stopped to talk to us while I was taking Destiny for a walk, and when he reached out to give me a check for Mom and Dad, Destiny bit him," Abby muttered, slumping her shoulders and fiddling with the end of Destiny's leash. She knew this was probably it for Destiny—her parents wouldn't allow an aggressive dog to stay at the ranch. "Well, she actually bit his watch, so I don't think she hurt him. But she could have."

"She seems pretty calm now," Grace said, looking at Destiny, who was still trying to frolic with Blue.

Emily looked thoughtful. "How were you feeling when you were talking to Mr. Jackson, Abby?"

"Actually, I was really freaked out by some dogs that had leaped out and startled us on the way there. I didn't really want to talk to Mr. Jackson at all."

"Hmm," Emily said. "If you were really feeling that upset, Destiny might have thought you were in danger."

"That's true," Abby said, straightening up. "I was pretty much on the verge of a meltdown. From my body language, Destiny probably thought Mr. Jackson was attacking me."

"And that's not really the same as biting someone without warning," Emily said. "Even Amigo might bite someone if he thought you were being hurt. Destiny just misread the signals."

The next day, Abby rode her bike to the feed store. Her parents had wanted her to apologize to Mr. Jackson. Even though she dreaded going back there, Abby knew it was the right thing to do. And it was her idea to bring the money she had saved from her allowance. She explained to Mr. Jackson about the training she had been doing with Destiny, and offered to pay for his watch, but he refused it.

"It seems like that dog still has some things left to learn," he said. "But don't worry about the watch. I figure it was due to be replaced. Durn thing got pretty annoying, in fact—always seemed to think I was running late!" Mr. Jackson let out one of his booming laughs and offered Abby an old-fashioned lemon drop from the jar of candy next to the cash register. Abby thanked him and scurried out of the store, relieved that he wasn't going to sue her family or ban them from shopping there.

"You and Amigo be sure to stop by again real

soon!" he called after her. He didn't say anything about Destiny stopping by, and Abby didn't blame him.

"It does sound like Destiny was trying to defend you," Miriam said the next day at lunchtime. "Especially if she met the postal worker and all those other people and doesn't even bark at them at all."

"Yeah, she's actually getting really friendly with our mail carrier now," Abby said. "And I'm still trying to introduce her to as many people as possible—just only when I'm in a good mood myself. Hey, do you want to come over after school and meet her?"

"I can't today," Miriam said, sounding disappointed. "I have to leave early for an appointment. Caleb's going to see a counselor, and the whole family is supposed to be there for the first session."

Abby nodded, crunching down on a baby carrot. Seeing Destiny eat so many of them had given Abby a craving for them lately. "LeeAnn has helped me with a lot of stuff, especially since Amigo stopped coming to school with me."

"I hope it helps," Miriam said. "A few days ago he had another big argument with my parents. I'm not even sure what it was about. But I heard shouting, and then he slammed the door and left, and didn't come home until the next day. My parents said that if he wants to keep living with us, he has to get help."

Miriam sighed, stirring cinnamon into a cup of the cafeteria's rice pudding. "Honestly, I'm kind of surprised that he even agreed to go, considering how weird he's been acting. Sometimes it doesn't feel like he's my brother at all anymore."

Abby nodded. "I saw a trailer for a new sci-fi movie about people being taken over by little alien bugs that crawl into their ears and totally change their personality," she said. Then she realized that probably wasn't the most helpful response. "But I doubt that's what happened to Caleb," she added.

"Oh, Abby!" Miriam laughed so hard that she nearly snorted rice pudding out her nose. "I guess that's one thing to be thankful for."

After school, Abby vacuumed the entire downstairs of the house. It wasn't one of her regular chores, but the vacuum was on her list of things Destiny needed to get used to.

When Abby dragged the vacuum cleaner out of the closet, Destiny ran and hid under the table. But Destiny soon learned that the machine did more than make a loud noise and suck up any object in its path. Now it was also a treat dispenser.

First, Destiny met the silent vacuum cleaner and snatched a carrot from where it had been placed in the vacuum's path. For the second carrot, Destiny had to approach the running vacuum to get her treat.

The session went a little too well. By the end of it, Destiny was dancing so close to Abby as she worked that she nearly *did* get vacuumed up—or her tail, at least.

When Abby was finished, she checked "vacuum cleaners" off Destiny's training list and realized she had reached the end of it. Destiny had now been exposed and desensitized to nearly everything that had scared her before. She'd been very carefully reintroduced to the kittens under Emily's supervision, and to Mr. Jackson when he stopped by with a new brand of rabbit feed. A few baby carrots later, Mr. Jackson had joined Destiny's rapidly growing list of friends.

The only thing left that Abby could think of was Destiny's strange fear of cheese. And that wasn't exactly something that would interfere with Destiny's safety or quality of life, so Abby decided to leave it alone. She figured dogs were allowed to have preferences just like people did.

Besides, baby carrots were probably a healthier treat. And they had definitely been an effective reward. Destiny didn't even cringe as Abby rolled the heavy vacuum cleaner past on her way to put it back in the closet.

Then, inspiration struck Abby. If she could train Destiny to relax in situations that had scared her before, why couldn't Abby do the same thing for herself?

Chapter Seven

Abby grabbed a notebook and her laptop and went into her Cave of Solitude so no one would interrupt her train of thought. An hour later, she emerged with a plan.

But she would need help to pull it off. Who could she ask? Miriam would probably be happy to help, but Abby only got to see her at school and occasionally on weekends. Her parents knew a lot about animal training, but they were so busy. Natalie would probably be willing to help, too, but she could be a little bossy and would almost definitely end up totally revising Abby's plan, trying to make it "better."

That left two options. Abby headed out to the barn and found her younger sisters untacking their ponies. Abby kept her distance . . . Horses were beautiful, but their snorty breath and unpredictable hooves made her nervous.

"Emily and Grace," she said, "I have a favor to ask you."

"What is it?" Emily asked, unbuckling Bluebonnet's girth and sliding the saddle off the horse's back.

"I need you to help train me not to be afraid of the beach," Abby said matter-of-factly.

Grace burst out laughing so hard that she startled

her pony, Joker. "Oh, Abby, I know you love dogs, but that's just silly. What do you want us to do? Give you a biscuit and a belly rub?"

"No," Abby said, "I need you to help desensitize me to all the things that bother me about the beach, one by one."

"Desensitize?" Grace asked, scrunching up her face in confusion.

"Get used to," Abby explained. "I can't talk myself out of feeling freaked out, but I can expose myself to each situation little by little, the way I'm teaching Destiny not to be scared of men and kittens and vacuums and stuff."

Grace was still chuckling to herself, but Emily looked curious. "You really think the same kind of training can help a person?" she asked.

"I think so," Abby said, "but I can't do it by myself."

Grace finally stopped laughing. "I still think it sounds weird, but if it'll get you to come to the beach with the rest of us, I'll help you."

"Me too," Emily added.

"Thanks," Abby said. "I already have a program written up. We can start with the first item on the list tomorrow."

"What's up first?" asked Emily, gathering up Bluebonnet's saddle and bridle to carry them back to the tack room.

Abby sighed. "Buy a bathing suit I don't hate," she said. She was already loathing the idea.

"What do you think of this one, Abby?" Emily held up a lemon-yellow two-piece bathing suit with a frilly skirt.

"It's so bright," Abby said, squinting. It was hard to even look directly at it—Abby felt like the color might sear her eyes, as if she were staring at the sun.

"Of course it is! It's a bathing suit!" said Grace. "But on the other hand, you might want a one-piece for the beach. Remember last year's Great Bikini Disaster?"

"I couldn't forget it," Abby said. She hadn't actually been there, but she had heard all about it. Natalie had gotten a new two-piece bathing suit that apparently hadn't tied on too securely. The first time a big wave had washed over her, it had taken the top of her bathing suit with it. A *boy* had brought it back to her. According to Emily and Grace, he had been cute and had totally kept his head turned away, but Natalie had been too embarrassed even to thank him.

Thinking about the story gave Abby yet another item to add to her anti-beach list. "Let's go with a one-piece," she said to Emily and Grace.

"What about this?" Grace asked, grabbing a suit covered in giant hot-pink roses.

"Ugh," Abby said. "I don't like ugly flowers any better than Natalie does. I don't think anyone likes them. Why do they even make bathing suits with such stupid fabric?" Abby was starting to feel crabby from department-store overload. The fluorescent lights were flickering overhead, and the jumble of neon bathing suits seemed to swim in front of her eyes.

Then she spotted a bit of plain dark-blue cloth. She tugged at it and found a simple navy bathing suit with a double row of white stripes up each side.

And it was her size. "Mission accomplished," she said. "Can we go now?"

But Emily, Grace, and Natalie hadn't picked out bathing suits for themselves yet. After what felt like an eternity, Emily found a bathing suit with a cute paw-print pattern. Natalie selected a one-piece—of course—in a pretty aqua color. Grace decided to risk a two-piece because she found one with a shimmery fish-scale pattern that she couldn't resist.

They met Mrs. Ramirez at the cash register, and she paid for the suits, along with a wide-brimmed sun hat for herself and a couple of new beach towels. Most of their old ones had been turned into dog-drying or cat-warming or bunny-wrapping towels.

Later, as Abby checked the first item off her list, she felt a sense of accomplishment. Of course, picking a bathing suit was the easy part. The real work would begin after school tomorrow.

Overnight, a heat wave swept over central Texas. Even though it was still late May, it was over ninety degrees by noon.

"How was your family's appointment with the counselor?" Abby asked Miriam during recess as they sat in the shade of a cypress tree on the school playground. It still wasn't very cool, but it was better than being out on the hot ball field or metal playground equipment.

"Good, I think," said Miriam. "The therapist said that Caleb has something called post-traumatic stress disorder. I guess that means he had to see and do a lot of really difficult things in the army, and it's hard for him to let those memories go, even though he's safe now."

"That makes sense," Abby said. "I can't even watch movies about war on TV. It must be a million times worse to go through it for real."

"Yeah," said Miriam. "I was kind of hoping Caleb would talk to me about what happened—and, you know, realize that I'm old enough to understand. But the therapist said it might not be helpful for him or for me. I still kind of wish I knew what exactly happened, but on the other hand, I kind of don't want to know."

For some reason, what Miriam said made Abby think of Destiny. Sometimes people—even Miriam— got annoyed when Abby changed the subject to dogs from something else, but she was pretty sure there was a connection.

"I feel the same way about what happened to Destiny," she said. "When she first came to the ranch, I really wished I knew what had happened to her to make her so afraid. But I think that knowing the details would have just made me angry. And I was

able to help her anyway, by helping her make better memories."

"Do you think when Caleb's back for long enough, the good memories of being home will replace the bad ones?" Miriam asked.

"I don't know," Abby said. "I'm better at figuring out dogs than people." She still wondered if her training program for herself would work. She'd been worrying about it all day, so much so that she'd missed four out of ten questions on her math quiz—and she was usually good at math.

"I think you're better at figuring out people than you realize," Miriam said.

No one had ever said anything like that to Abby before. Was it possible that dogs and people weren't really that different after all?

Chapter Eight

Abby took off her shoes and walked barefoot across the scorching hot driveway. *It isn't really scalding my feet like hot lava*, she told herself.

When she reached the other side, Grace gave her a gummy bear. They were Abby's favorite treat—the equivalent of Destiny's baby carrots.

"Good doggie, Abby," Grace said with a giggle as she handed over the candy. Clearly, she still thought Abby's idea was silly. But Emily and Grace had both given up their riding time to help her.

"By pairing something bad, like walking on a hot road, with something good, like eating a gummy bear, I should stop minding it so much," Abby explained to Grace. "It's called 'classical conditioning.'"

Abby walked one more time across the driveway to make her point. Hot sand, check. The beach couldn't possibly be hotter than the sunbaked driveway.

Next, Abby lay on a towel on the lawn and asked Grace to spray a hose next to her, so that cold droplets splattered all over her skin. Grace sat next to Abby and gave her a gummy bear every fifteen seconds. Cold ocean spray, check.

After a while, the gummy bears started to melt into a blob in Emily's hand, and Abby was starting

to get a stomachache from eating so many of them. She signaled to Grace to turn off the hose.

"I think that's enough for now," she said.

"Besides, if you keep eating gummy bears, you might actually associate them with all this nasty stuff and stop liking them," said Grace. "And your plan would totally backfire, and that would be tragic."

She had a point. Abby didn't even want to look at a gummy bear right now. But at least she had more or less gotten used to the different situations that might take place at the beach.

After that, Abby and Grace played loud pop music that Abby didn't like and threw a basketball back and forth over Abby's chair as she sat reading a book. They didn't have a beach ball at home. Abby only got hit in the head with the ball once, and she even managed not to throttle Emily for accidentally dropping it on her.

"Maybe this isn't going to be so hard after all," Abby said.

The next day, Abby sat in LeeAnn's office, squeezing a stress ball. Her mom would be there in a few minutes to take her home.

It had been a bad day from the time Abby had gotten up and discovered they were out of both bananas *and* peanut butter. It was as if she had used up all her patience on her training program the day before and had had nothing left to deal with everyday annoyances.

She hadn't exactly *meant* to throw the book at Jamal Parker. But during free-reading time in the library, Jamal had kept making cartoon noises out loud as he'd read his comic book, saying stuff like "Pow!" and "Blam!" every few seconds.

Abby had walked up to Jamal, tapped him on the shoulder, and said, "Please read silently so that other people can concentrate." Then she'd gone back to her chair.

Jamal had stopped making comic book noises. Instead, he'd started saying, "Please read silently so that other people can concentrate," over and over again to his friends in an annoying robot voice.

The next thing Abby knew, the book was sailing out of her hands. If she had been reading a chapter book or a comic, it might not have been a big deal. But Abby had been reading *The Encyclopedia of Dogs*, a 572-page hardcover. The corner of the book had left a red mark on Jamal's arm. Not even an actual scrape, but Jamal had been a real baby about it.

The school's zero-tolerance policy for fighting meant that Abby had to be sent home for the day. It didn't seem fair. She thought that mocking someone in a robot voice was nearly as bad as throwing a book at them, and Jamal had only gotten a warning.

In the car, Mrs. Ramirez didn't lecture her like Abby was half-expecting. But Abby almost wished she would. Instead, her mom just asked, "What would help you calm down this afternoon?"

"I'm already calm," Abby muttered. And it was true—this hadn't been a real meltdown like she used to have, where everything felt totally out of control. She was pretty sure she could have stopped herself from throwing the book at Jamal if she'd really wanted to.

When they got home, Abby went right to her Cave of Solitude. But the blue walls surrounding her made her think of the ocean, which reminded her of the family's upcoming vacation. If Abby couldn't get through a regular day at school, how could she possibly handle a whole day at the noisy, crowded beach?

She might as well leave her new bathing suit at home and face the fact that there were some situations she just couldn't deal with.

Later, her mom came up to her room while Abby was watching a Cesar Millan episode about an overprotective Akita that chased visitors into his family's swimming pool. At least Destiny wasn't that bad!

Abby didn't really feel like talking, so for a minute, she kept watching the video and pretended she didn't see her mom standing there. Then she pretended she didn't hear her mom calling her name. But when "Abby" changed to "Abigail Luisa," Abby paused the video and looked up at her mom.

"What is it?" Abby asked. She sort of wished she had stayed in her Cave of Solitude where no one could bother her.

Her mom sat down on the edge of Abby's bed. "It seems like you've been having some trouble lately, especially since Amigo stopped going to school with you," she said.

Abby nodded reluctantly. Today had been the worst, but her grades had been dropping a little for the entire year, and she'd gotten a couple of warnings for arguing with other students or not listening to her teacher.

"I know the trip to Florida has been stressing you out, and your dad and I were wondering if maybe you'd rather stay home this year," her mom said. "Marco's family said they'd be happy to stay here with you for the week, if you wanted."

Abby thought for a moment. It was true that she found vacations kind of overwhelming, but she didn't want to miss the whole trip. Her family always did fun stuff while they were in Florida. Last year, they'd all gone to watch a dog agility trial. She didn't want to be stuck in Texas doing all her usual chores—plus everyone else's—while the rest of her family was having a great time.

"I want to go on the trip," Abby said finally. "Amigo and I will just hang out at the condo like usual. Maybe I'll even go to the beach one of the days. That's what I've been planning."

Mrs. Ramirez bit her lip. "Honey, I don't think Amigo should come with us this year," she said.

"What?!" Abby screeched. "But he can't miss our vacation. He's part of the family!"

"I know he is, but we have to consider what's best for him," Mrs. Ramirez said. "You know he hasn't been feeling too energetic lately, and a trip to Florida would be quite stressful for him."

At first, Abby wanted to argue. She needed Amigo with her if she was going to survive the week! Then she thought about what her mom had said. She'd never forgive herself if something happened to Amigo because they made him take a long trip away from home while he needed to rest.

"You're right," Abby said finally. "If Amigo's not going to enjoy the trip, I don't want him to go." She thought about it for a moment. "But I still want to go," she said and paused again. "Could Destiny come with us instead?"

Mrs. Ramirez started shaking her head before Abby even finished her sentence. "I think Destiny's got a long way to go before she's ready for a long-distance trip like this."

"I know, but there's two weeks before the trip," Abby said. "She'll be ready by then." Silently she added, *And so will I.*

Chapter Nine

"This was a good idea, Abby," Grace said as Mrs. Ramirez tried to find a parking space in the crowded lot. "If you can survive a day at the Sugarberry town pool, you can survive anything." The car braked sharply as a couple of kids in swim gear darted out from behind a minivan.

"Not to mention it's extra-crazy since it's the opening weekend and roasting hot outside," she added.

"What do you think, Abby?" Emily asked, gathering up their beach bag full of towels. "Are you sure you're up for it?"

Even in the parking lot, the smell of chlorine was overpowering. *But it's no worse than the fishy smells from the beach will be*, Abby reminded herself.

"Let's do it," she said.

When they got to the pool area, Abby's mom put on her new sun hat and headed over to the shaded lounge chairs to read her new mystery novel. Emily and Grace tossed their towels over a couple of chairs and headed for the pool.

"Wait!" ordered Emily, holding up a purple bottle. "Sunscreen."

Abby shuddered as Emily smeared the slimy glop

all over her back, but she knew that having a painful sunburn would be worse.

Once they were all coated in the greasy stuff, Grace dived right in to the deep end of the pool while Emily climbed down the ladder and glided across the water in a smooth backstroke. Abby went around to the shallow end, with the little kids, and dipped her toe in the water. It wasn't too cold, actually.

Abby lowered her blue goggles over her eyes and took two steps into the pool, up to her knees. She waited as her legs adjusted to the temperature. She took a third step down, up to her waist, and crossed her arms in front of her. Finally, she took a big breath and launched off the steps, careful to keep her head above water. Abby hated to get her hair wet when she went swimming.

She doggie paddled past a couple of kids playing with a set of diving rings.

"Hey, no fair!" one of them shrieked at another. "You have to grab the ring with your hands, not your feet, or it doesn't count!"

"Says who?" the second one countered.

"Says Poseidon, vengeful god of the tides!" cried the first kid, and he spun around with his hands skimming the water so that a huge wave washed across the entire shallow end. Abby's hair was soaked.

At first, Abby wanted to splash the kid right back—or maybe dunk him. But then the lifeguard

would kick her out of the pool, and her mom would probably say Abby was too worked up to go on the trip to Florida.

Instead, Abby sank her head under the water and looked through her goggles at the grungy bottom of the pool. She could see bits of grass, leaves, a few old pennies, and some dead insects swirling around people's feet.

After that, Abby swam without touching the bottom because she was afraid of stepping on something gross. When she was tired, she got out of the water and lay on one of the beach chairs. The sun dried her instantly and then started to slowly bake her. Wrapped in her beach towel, Abby felt like an enchilada in an oven.

She took her iPod out of her beach bag and started listening to a podcast that she'd downloaded earlier about dog training. Even with the volume all the way up, she could hardly hear it over the sound of kids shrieking and splashing. Abby startled as a lifeguard let out a piercing whistle to stop a kid from diving into the shallow end—the same kid who'd splashed Abby earlier.

Emily and Grace came over a little while later with a handful of ice pops. "Here, we got one for you," said Emily, handing her a blue one. Abby took it gratefully and was dismayed to see that the ice pop was mostly melted in its plastic tube. She slurped up the sugary water anyway so that she wouldn't get dehydrated.

Mrs. Ramirez came over to where they were sitting. "I'm afraid we'll have to go, girls," she said. "I'm on call today, and I just got a message from Tina that Mrs. Lamar's cat, Tigger, has a blocked kidney stone. I'm going to need to operate on him this afternoon."

Abby was sorry to hear about Tigger but glad for the excuse to go. She needed to use the restroom, and she was tempted to just wait until they got home. But she wouldn't be able to do that at the beach in Florida. Abby took a deep breath and held it as she darted into the damp, dank bathroom, found the least disgusting empty stall, and after she was through, washed her hands with huge globs of slimy pink soap.

She emerged with a gasp, sucking in a huge lungful of chlorine-scented air.

"Are you okay?" Emily asked sympathetically. She hated the pool bathrooms too.

"I'm excellent," Abby said as they walked back to the car. "I survived exposure to slimy sunscreen, cold water, scorching sunlight, dead bugs in the pool, loud kids, and disgusting bathrooms. I guess there's nothing I can do about jellyfish or seagulls here in Texas."

"I could caw really loudly in your ear and steal your lunch," offered Grace.

"That's okay," Abby said. "I think I'm as ready as I'll ever be."

"I can't sit in the middle, or I'll get carsick," Abby said.

No one seemed to have heard her. Everyone was trying to fit the massive pile of luggage into the SUV. The sun hadn't even risen yet, but the family bustled about as if it were midday. They kept putting things in, rearranging them, and then taking them back out again.

Abby stood a little distance away, holding Destiny's leash. She kept looking up at Abby for reassurance, as if to ask where they were going so early in the morning. Abby wished she could explain it in words that Destiny could understand. She could still hardly believe she had convinced her parents to let Destiny go along with them. But they had been impressed with Abby's demonstration of Destiny trotting happily alongside Marco with a kitten on her back while he carried an umbrella and ran a vacuum cleaner across the kitchen floor.

"Be sure to leave a space for Destiny's crate!" called Abby as the car filled up. Her dad removed a stack of beach chairs in order to lift the large dog crate into the family's SUV, behind the two rows of back seats.

Finally, everything was packed, minus Emily's model horse collection, which Mr. and Mrs. Ramirez had vetoed in order to fit the beach chairs.

"We'll be too busy to play model horses anyway," Grace said.

Abby led Destiny over to the car. "Up, girl!" she said, patting the inside of the crate so Destiny would jump into it. Destiny gave Abby a quizzical look and then glanced longingly toward the house.

"Come on, girl." Abby tugged on Destiny's leash. Destiny crouched down onto her haunches and refused to budge.

"Maybe this isn't going to work," Mrs. Ramirez said.

Abby closed her eyes and made her mind clear and calm. She did two square breaths and opened her eyes. She took a baby carrot out of her back pocket and held it up.

"Let's go, Destiny!" Abby tossed the carrot into the crate. Destiny leaped up and scrambled after it. Abby quickly shut the door behind her. Destiny turned around in the small space and let out a nervous bark and then a high-pitched whine.

"Is she going to do that all the way to Florida?" Natalie asked, putting her hands over her ears. "It's way too early for all that racket."

"No," Abby said. She reached into her travel bag and pulled out her secret weapon: a rubber Kong toy filled with peanut butter.

Abby opened the crate door and set the Kong in front of Destiny. She sniffed at the toy and took a careful lick. Then she grabbed it with both her paws and was silent except for the slurping of peanut butter.

"I guess we're ready to go, then," Mrs. Ramirez said, looking a little surprised and very relieved. She got into the driver's seat for the first leg of their trip, and Mr. Ramirez settled in the other front seat. Natalie got to sit in the back row of seats by herself because the others were filled with luggage.

"I can't sit in the middle, or I'll get carsick," Abby said. Once again, no one was paying attention.

Abby climbed into the first row of back seats, and Emily got in next to her. Grace went around to the other side and slid in next to Abby, forcing her to scoot over.

"*I can't sit in the middle, or I'll get carsick!*" Abby screamed. Everyone heard her that time.

"Okay! Jeez, you don't need to yell," Grace said. She scrambled over Abby's lap into the middle seat, and Abby moved over to the window.

"Everyone buckled up?" their mom asked.

"Everyone except Destiny," Abby said. "But she can't wear a seat belt, so please drive carefully and don't crash."

"I'll do my best," her mom promised, checking the rearview camera to make sure none of the outdoor cats had wandered behind the SUV. She backed down the driveway, and they were off!

It seemed to take forever for them just to get out of town, never mind out of Texas. For the first few hours, everyone was quiet, watching the sun rise and listening to a book on CD. Then Emily and Grace started to dig into the snack supply. Abby covered her ears to drown out the deafening sound of Grace crunching her cheesy chips.

"Could you please not chew so loudly?" Abby asked when she couldn't take it anymore.

"I'm not chewing loudly," Grace said indignantly. "*This* is chewing loudly." She demonstrated.

The trip to Florida took fifteen hours, with a couple of quick bathroom breaks for Abby's family and Destiny. The trip felt infinite to Abby. But finally, the car's headlights shone on the cozy stucco condo that would be their home for the next week. The air was so humid that Abby felt as if she were swimming as she went around back to let Destiny out of her crate.

Across the street, Abby saw the downtown boardwalk lined with palm trees and heard the distant crash of the ocean. From a distance, the sound was almost soothing.

Abby took Destiny for a walk around the yard to do her business while her parents and sisters brought

all their luggage inside. Destiny seemed curious about her new surroundings but not frightened. She sniffed at a bush covered with magenta blossoms. The scent of flowers perfumed the whole night air.

Then Destiny let out a yelp of surprise. Abby looked around for what had scared Destiny and laughed when she saw a tiny frog hopping away into the garden.

"Come on, girl, let's go inside," Abby said. "Let's just hope you're not scared of the plastic flamingos on the porch!"

On the first day of vacation, Abby's family didn't go to the beach at all. Instead, they went to a horse show.

A few months before, a Paint horse named Tango had come to the ranch. Natalie had developed a special bond with Tango and had decided to keep him and train him as a barrel-racing horse. But it turned out that he had been stolen from his real owner, a teenage girl named Rachel who lived in Florida and rode him English, not Western.

Natalie had been sad to give up Tango, but she had kept in touch with Rachel. When Natalie had told Rachel about their trip to Florida, Rachel had invited them all to watch a show that she and Tango were competing in.

The horse show was quite noisy and dusty, but it was better than the beach. And it was exciting to watch the horses jump over courses of big fences decorated with stripes, flowers, and even pools of water. There were lots of tight turns and difficult combination jumps. Some horses knocked down fences or had refusals. One rider even fell off. But Rachel and

Tango cleared everything with ease. They ended up winning third place out of twenty-six horses.

The next day, Abby convinced everyone to go to Animal Kingdom. Emily even got picked to help an elephant and its trainer. Grace was so jealous that she wouldn't speak to Emily for most of the day—but then she ended up winning a raffle for a giant stuffed gorilla, which cheered her up.

The third day, there was no escape. Abby suggested they all go to a movie, but no one was interested. Everyone changed into their bathing suits, slathered on the sunscreen, and packed a big cooler full of drinks and food.

Destiny had to stay at the condo, and Abby was really tempted to keep her company. But Destiny looked perfectly happy lying on the rug in the air-conditioned living room. She had adjusted to being in Florida better than anyone could have hoped for, and Abby felt determined to do the same.

Chapter Ten

"Wow, this place is a zoo," Mrs. Ramirez said. "Where should we set up our chairs?"

"Somewhere nearby, please," said Emily, who was struggling to carry the heavy cooler.

Abby would have helped her, but her own arms were filled with beach chairs.

They had arrived pretty late, since Grace had somehow lost one of her flip-flops, and they'd had to stop at a nearby gift shop to get her a new pair. The beach was already covered with colorful chairs, umbrellas, and towels.

Finally, Natalie spotted a small open patch about halfway down the beach. They all wound through the obstacle course of sunbathers, sandcastle-builders, joggers, and volleyball players until they reached it.

Their neighbors on one side were playing loud music from wireless speakers. On their other side, a baby was crying. But Abby was prepared. She took a striped towel out of her beach bag and laid it carefully in the shade of the umbrella her parents had set up. She put on a pair of sunglasses, took a book out of her bag, and started to read—keeping a wary eye on a pair of seagulls that landed nearby.

One by one, Abby's family headed off to the water.

Grace and Emily went first, followed by Natalie, and finally, their parents. Abby was left all alone under the umbrella. Well, more shade for her. Abby turned a page of her book. The wind blew it back, along with a lot of sand. Abby wiped her forehead, and her arm came away covered in beads of sweat and grit.

The ocean seemed almost inviting now. Abby kicked off her sandals, set down her sunglasses, and headed for the water. She walked in up to her ankles. The water was cold but not any colder than the town pool in Texas.

She looked down and saw a school of silvery fish darting around her feet.

From a distance the ocean was bluish-green, but when Abby stared directly into it, the color was almost golden. Abby wondered why that was; she'd have to look it up later.

Abby drifted deeper and deeper into the water. Suddenly, she felt the tide rush back away from her. A cool, shadowy feeling fell over her, and she looked up to see a huge wave heading toward her.

She barely had time to take a deep breath before it hit her, knocking her off her feet. Abby was dragged along the rough ocean floor. Seaweed wrapped itself like strong ropes around her arms and legs.

Abby washed up on the shore with a gasp. She pushed herself up onto her hands and coughed up the water she'd swallowed. A guy with a surfboard

stopped in front of her and said, "Dude, that was a gnarly wave. Are you okay?"

Abby nodded, and the guy kept walking. But she didn't feel okay. Her arms and legs stung from being scraped on the rough sand. She was covered in seaweed, and a little crab was clinging to her bathing suit. Abby looked around, but she didn't see anyone in her family. Nothing was familiar, and all the strangers on the beach seemed to be laughing at her.

Abby could feel a meltdown coming on. It wasn't just like getting upset and throwing a book or raising her voice. It was a helpless, chaotic feeling that washed over her as intensely as that giant wave and left her mind and body totally out of control.

Abby felt hot tears sliding down her cheeks, and her breath caught in her throat. Her legs felt like jelly, too weak even for her to stand up and pick the slimy seaweed out of her hair.

Abby squeezed her eyes shut and blocked out the hot sun and the cold water and the caws of seagulls and the sound of laughter. She pictured herself at home in her Cave of Solitude, except Amigo was with her. She knew he would always be there for her. She hugged him, and he licked her face.

Abby opened her eyes. The slobbery feeling was actually a piece of seaweed sliding off her head and down her face. She picked it off and threw it back into the ocean, along with the tiny crab and the other various ocean plants that were wrapped around her like a mummy's bandages. Then she took a few deep breaths, got to her feet, and looked around until she saw her family's yellow-and-white-striped beach umbrella.

She walked over to it across a desert of burning sand and sat in one of the beach chairs, which promptly collapsed under her weight. Abby tossed the chair aside and sat on her towel instead.

She looked around the beach until she spotted her mom with Grace and Emily, standing in a long line for the restrooms. She looked in the other direction and found her dad jogging along the edge of the water. Natalie was harder to locate, but Abby finally spied her chatting with a couple of teenagers, including a boy who looked kind of like Marco.

Well, that was just great—at least the rest of her family was having fun. Abby figured a cold drink might help take the salty seawater taste out of her mouth. She reached for the cooler and discovered that someone had left the top off, so the ice had melted. Abby reached into the soupy water and pulled out a lukewarm bottle of lemonade.

A group of seagulls had seen her grab the bottle, and they gathered around in a big circle. Abby threw a handful of sand at them, and they fluttered back a few feet. But they didn't go away.

Abby stood up and started to walk down the beach

to get away from them, bringing her lemonade with her. She found that it was easier to walk close to the water, where the sand was wet and packed firm. She spotted a pretty scalloped shell with pink and purple inside and picked it up. Abby wondered if Miriam would like it. Shells weren't exactly rocks or gemstones, but they were pretty.

She spotted another shell a little way down the beach. This one was oval-shaped and iridescent inside. She gulped down the last of the lemonade, rinsed out the bottle, and started using it to collect shells. She found one that was long and spiraled, like a unicorn's horn, and another that was spotted, like a tortoiseshell cat. She even found a tiny starfish.

"Hey!"

Abby turned and saw a boy with a mask of sunscreen over his freckled nose holding up a beach ball. She froze. Was he going to whack her upside the head with it like the last time Abby had gone to the beach?

"We need one more person for a volleyball team," said the boy. "Want to play?"

The other players ended up being the boy's sisters. They were identical twins, like Emily and Grace. Their family was from Minnesota.

The volleyball game was fun, even though Abby and the boy, David, lost against his sisters. Somehow, meeting kids at the beach hadn't been as awkward as meeting them around town or in a new classroom.

Abby heard someone calling her name and turned to see her parents waving to her from farther down the shoreline. Her sisters were packing up the umbrella and chairs. To her surprise, Abby felt disappointed. She said goodbye to David and his sisters and ran back across the beach to where her family was waiting.

Back at the condo, everyone showered and rested for a few hours before heading out to dinner at a restaurant overlooking the water. It specialized in seafood, but the cook was happy to make Abby a plain hamburger and a lemonade, which were both actually quite tasty.

Later that evening, the family took Destiny out for a stroll along the boardwalk. She stayed close to Abby's side but sniffed curiously at the people passing by. When a big man with a lot of tattoos declared himself a German shepherd lover and stooped down to pat her, she didn't even bark or growl.

The family stopped at an ice-cream cart for dessert, and everyone got chocolate-dipped cones—except for Abby, who got vanilla soft serve in a dish, and Grace, who insisted on ordering a sundae with pineapple sauce and gummy bears.

"Look familiar, Abby?" Grace asked, offering Abby one of the candies.

Abby shuddered. Grace had been right—she still couldn't stomach another gummy bear after her training program. But at least the program had worked! Even with the tidal wave, the beach still hadn't been as bad as she'd expected.

"Hey, look!" Emily had spotted a section of beach where pets were allowed. It was rockier than the beach where they'd spent the day, and the waves crashed more roughly against the shore.

When Abby led Destiny toward the water, the dog hesitated. Abby felt her start to tremble.

"It's okay," Abby said, walking a little bit ahead of Destiny so she could see there was no danger. Abby walked until she was ankle-deep in the water and could feel the cold spray on her face.

The leash between them was stretched taut until Destiny put one cautious paw on the wet sand, then another. Then she bounded along the shoreline and dragged Abby out of the water and down the beach, sniffing at everything and rooting her nose into the sand. She even growled and snapped playfully at the water as if it were another dog.

"I guess it wasn't Destiny's destiny to be such a scaredy-pup," Emily said, giggling, once the rest of the family had caught up to Abby.

"There have been a lot of changes in that dog, and it's all thanks to you, Abby," Mr. Ramirez said. "If I hadn't seen it for myself, I'm not sure I would have believed it was possible."

"And Destiny isn't the only one making progress," Mrs. Ramirez said. "I'm really proud of you for pushing yourself outside your comfort zone."

"So did you actually have fun at the beach today?" Natalie asked, as they started back home.

"Sort of," Abby said. "Except for being dragged underwater by an epic tidal wave. That will never be in my comfort zone. But I found a lot of shells for Miriam, and I had fun playing volleyball. I still don't like seagulls, though."

"Me neither," Emily said. "I made the mistake of giving one of them a cheesy chip, and then they followed me everywhere."

"If I were a bird, I'd be a seagull," Grace said.

"I could fly across the ocean to visit any country I wanted and poop on the heads of everyone I don't like!" She cackled and ran down the boardwalk with her arms outstretched, probably imagining herself giving seagull-style revenge to the cheating players of the Sassafras Springs soccer team.

"So what are we going to do tomorrow?" Emily asked.

"Let's go to Disney World!" shouted Grace, dropping the seagull act.

"Not me," Natalie said. "If you kids want to go, that's fine, but I am way too old for Mickey Mouse and Princess Elsa. Anyway, I'd rather go to the beach again."

They decided that their dad would take Emily and Grace to Disney World, and their mom would go with Natalie to the beach.

"What do you want to do, Abby?" her mom asked.

Abby thought for a minute. Roller coasters and crowds and people dressed up in cartoon outfits sounded even more overwhelming than the beach. She'd sort of had fun today, but she was tired, and she wasn't sure that she'd have such a good time tomorrow.

"Can I stay at the condo and hang out with Destiny?" she asked. "I'm old enough to be by myself for a couple of hours now."

"I think that would be okay," her dad said. "And

maybe the day after tomorrow, we can all go on a whale-watching tour."

"Sounds good to me," Abby said.

The next day, the rest of the family left right after breakfast. Abby lay on the living room couch with Destiny and read a book about the Everglades that she'd found in a gift shop near the beach. Then she went outside and identified all the flowers and trees in the backyard. She played fetch with Destiny until they were both out of breath, and then they went back inside and cooled off with an ice pop for Abby and a couple of ice cubes for Destiny.

As far as Abby was concerned, it was the perfect way to spend an afternoon. The only thing that would have made it better was if Amigo had been there to enjoy it too.

Chapter Eleven

Four days later, Abby yawned and stepped out of the car onto the familiar dusty driveway of Second Chance Ranch. Instead of ocean spray and exotic flowers, Abby smelled parched grass and the earthy scent of cattle. Instead of crashing waves and seagulls, she heard the hum of a tractor and the cackle of chickens.

Abby let Destiny out of the car and ran straight into the house without bothering with her suitcase. She had something she wanted to do before it got too dark. Amigo was waiting for her at the door. He woofed with joy when he saw Abby and wagged his tail so hard that his whole hind end shimmied from side to side.

"Want to go for a walk, buddy?" she asked Amigo.

Destiny answered with a bark of her own, but Abby said, "Later, okay?," and gave her a couple of ice cubes, which were her new favorite treat.

Abby wanted some time alone with Amigo. She had missed him every day of the trip. Marco had even put him on FaceTime for a few minutes when the family had called to check in, but it hadn't been the same as really seeing him.

Abby took Amigo for a long walk around the ranch—through the horse pasture and up to the ridge that overlooked the neighboring cattle ranch. The sun was setting, bathing the rugged landscape in brilliant pink-and-orange light.

Abby sat on the ground next to Amigo and put her arm around him, pressing her cheek against his soft golden fur. The trip to Florida had been fun, but nothing could compare to being home in Texas with the dog who had helped to open the entire world for her.

"Here's a container of puppy food to get you started, Mr. Clark," said Abby. "Remember, Cinnamon should eat this for the first year before you transition to regular dog food. She's been doing well with her housebreaking, and we're working on voice commands like 'sit' and 'stay.' If you practice them a little bit every day, they should stick soon."

"Thank you, Miss Abby," said Cinnamon's new owner, who lived in a retirement complex in the middle of town. "I'm eternally grateful for your matchmaking services."

When Mr. Clark had first stopped by Second Chance Ranch, he had been determined to adopt Clove, another of Cocoa's puppies. But Clove was very hyper and liked to chew on furniture if he got bored. He wasn't a good match for someone living in a small apartment. So Abby had instead convinced Mr. Clark to adopt Cinnamon, a puppy with a calmer temperament.

The puppies were finally old enough to leave their mom. Abby helped Mr. Clark bundle Cinnamon into the puppy carrier and set it in the back of Mr. Clark's car. Just as he drove away, another car pulled into the driveway. Abby wondered if it was Clove's new owner, a park ranger who loved camping and trail running. The woman had said she would be stopping by to take Clove home this afternoon.

Instead, Abby saw that the visitors were Caleb and Miriam. She hadn't known they were planning to visit today. She waved and jogged over to greet them.

"Caleb was just driving me over to see his new apartment, and we decided to stop by here for the open house," said Miriam as Caleb helped her out of the front seat and into her wheelchair. He was wearing dark sunglasses, a black T-shirt, and heavy black boots. To Abby, it still looked like he was kind of mad or upset about something, but he said "hi" to her in a normal voice and didn't seem like he was going to yell again.

"Cool," Abby said. "Cinnamon just left, but you can see the rest of Cocoa's puppies—and visit Amigo, of course."

Abby and Miriam headed for the house, but Caleb wanted to see the horses, so he said he'd meet up with them later.

Miriam squealed with joy when she saw Amigo, and Amigo leaped to his feet to welcome her.

"Hey, how come *I* don't get a greeting like that every day?" Abby asked.

Amigo laid his head adoringly in Miriam's lap and slobbered all over her jeans. Miriam didn't seem to mind.

"Caleb's been doing better lately," she said to Abby,

stroking Amigo's forehead and smoothing the three little wrinkles between his eyes. "He got a job at the computer store in town, and he's renting a house with a couple of guys he went to high school with. Oh, and he finally figured out that I've got decent taste in movies now. We went to see the new James Bond last weekend!"

"Really? Your parents let you see it?" Abby asked. "Mine wouldn't because it's rated PG-13, and neither of them had time to go with me."

"Oh, my parents weren't going to let me see it, but Caleb agreed to take me if I promised not to tell them!" Miriam said with a wicked grin. "It finally feels like we're really brother and sister again, like old times. Well . . . almost. He still gets kind of angry sometimes and spends a lot of time in his room. But I think things are getting better."

"That's great," Abby said. "You're lucky that you have a brother who's old enough to drive you places. Natalie won't be that useful for, like, another four years."

"How was your family's trip to Florida?" Miriam asked. "Did you end up going to the beach?"

"Yes, and I brought back a bunch of shells for you." Abby ran up to her room and came back with her collection in the lemonade bottle. She poured the contents out onto an empty puzzle tray so Miriam could look at them.

"They're so cool," Miriam said, stirring the shells with her finger. "Look, a tiny starfish! And this one with the purple inside is amazing."

"I thought you might like them, even though they're not rocks or gemstones," Abby said, feeling pleased.

"I do," Miriam said. "I might have to start a new collection."

Miriam played with Amigo some more while Abby poured the shells back into the lemonade bottle so Miriam could take them home.

The kitchen door creaked open, and a moment later, Caleb strolled in. "Hey, Meerkat, you almost ready to go?" he asked Miriam.

"No!" she said, hugging Amigo around the neck.

"Can you stay for a few more minutes?" Abby asked. "You haven't met Destiny yet."

"Who's Destiny?" Caleb asked.

"Wait here!" Abby ran outside to the dog runs and came back with Destiny in tow.

"Wow, what an awesome German shepherd," said Caleb. "We had a couple of them in my regiment." For a moment, his eyes clouded over, and he seemed to be somewhere far away in his mind. Then he blinked and cleared his throat. "They're great dogs . . . loyal as can be."

Abby unclipped Destiny's leash so she could have free run of the room. Caleb spotted Destiny's rope toy on the floor, picked it up, and held it temptingly out to her.

Abby was a little worried that Destiny would be afraid of Caleb, with his deep voice and quick movements and big black boots. But after a moment of hesitation, Destiny opened her jaws and latched on to the toy, beginning a game of tug-of-war.

"She's so beautiful, Abby. Are you going to keep her?" Miriam asked, watching Caleb and Destiny play. It was hard to tell which of them was getting into the game more. Caleb dug in his heels and gently spun Destiny around in a circle. She hung on with determination, letting out little growls of concentration.

"I'm not sure," Abby said. "Destiny needs a lot of attention, and I've already got a dog. But it could be tough finding a home for her. She'll need someone who understands that she's been through a lot and can be patient with her."

Destiny succeeded in yanking the rope toy out of Caleb's hands. She paraded in a victory lap around the room, proudly holding it in her mouth. Caleb's face looked different now. He wasn't quite smiling, but almost.

"My new apartment allows pets, and I'm pretty sure my housemates would be cool with having a dog around," he said, his eyes on Destiny. "Maybe she could come live with me."

"Oh, perfect!" Miriam said. "You should definitely

adopt Destiny, Caleb. Then I can come visit, and it'll be almost like having a dog of my own." Miriam's face glowed with excitement, but Abby was more cautious. She always thought carefully before matching a dog with a new owner.

Destiny could still be challenging at times, and Caleb had never owned a dog before. Could he handle Destiny's behavior without scaring her or letting her get away with things?

Then Abby remembered what Miriam had said about Caleb having gone through a lot of tough situations in the army. Maybe he would understand Destiny better than most people. And maybe Destiny would be able to help him, the way Amigo had somehow known how to help Abby.

"What do you think, Desi? Wanna come hang out at my place and play Frisbee with the boys?" Caleb asked, crouching down and ruffling the thick fur on the back of Destiny's neck. She barked happily and wagged her tail, her eyes shining up at him.

Abby folded up Destiny's leash and handed it to Caleb. It didn't really matter what she thought—it was clear that Destiny had chosen her new owner for herself.

About the Author

Whitney Sanderson grew up riding horses as a member of a 4-H club and competing in local jumping and dressage shows. She has written several books in the Horse Diaries chapter book series. She is also the author of *Horse Rescue: Treasure*, based on her time volunteering at an equine rescue farm. She lives in Massachusetts.

About the Illustrator

Jomike Tejido is an author and illustrator who has illustrated the books *I Funny: School of Laughs* and *Middle School: Dog's Best Friend*, as well as the Pet Charms and I Want to Be . . . Dinosaurs! series. He has fond memories of horseback riding as a kid and has always liked drawing fluffy animals. Jomike lives in Manila with his wife, his daughter Sophia, and a chow chow named Oso.

Join Natalie, Abby, Emily, and Grace and
read more animal stories in . . .

BY KELSEY ABRAMS

ILLUSTRATED BY JOMIKE TEJIDO

CHARMING MIDDLE GRADE FICTION
FROM JOLLY FISH PRESS